To Nan and Frank

Library of Congress Cataloging-in-Publication Data available

ISBN 978-0-545-78892-2

10 9 8 7 6 5 4 3 2 1   15 16 17 18 19

Printed in China 108
First American edition, January 2015

Please, Mr. Panda

Steve Antony

Scholastic Press · New York

Would you like a doughnut?

Give me the pink one.

No, you cannot have a doughnut.
I have changed my mind.

Would you like a doughnut?

I want
the blue one
and
the yellow one.

No, you cannot have a doughnut.
I have changed my mind.

Would you like a doughnut?

Would you like a doughnut?

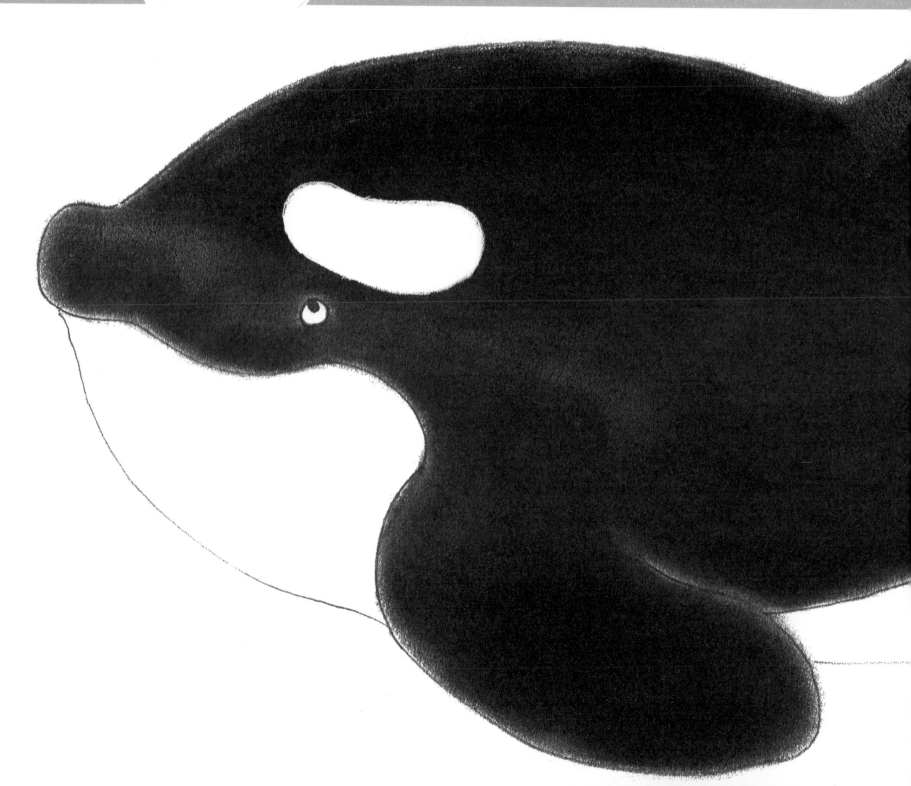

I want them all!

Then bring me some more.

No, you cannot have a doughnut.
I have changed my mind.

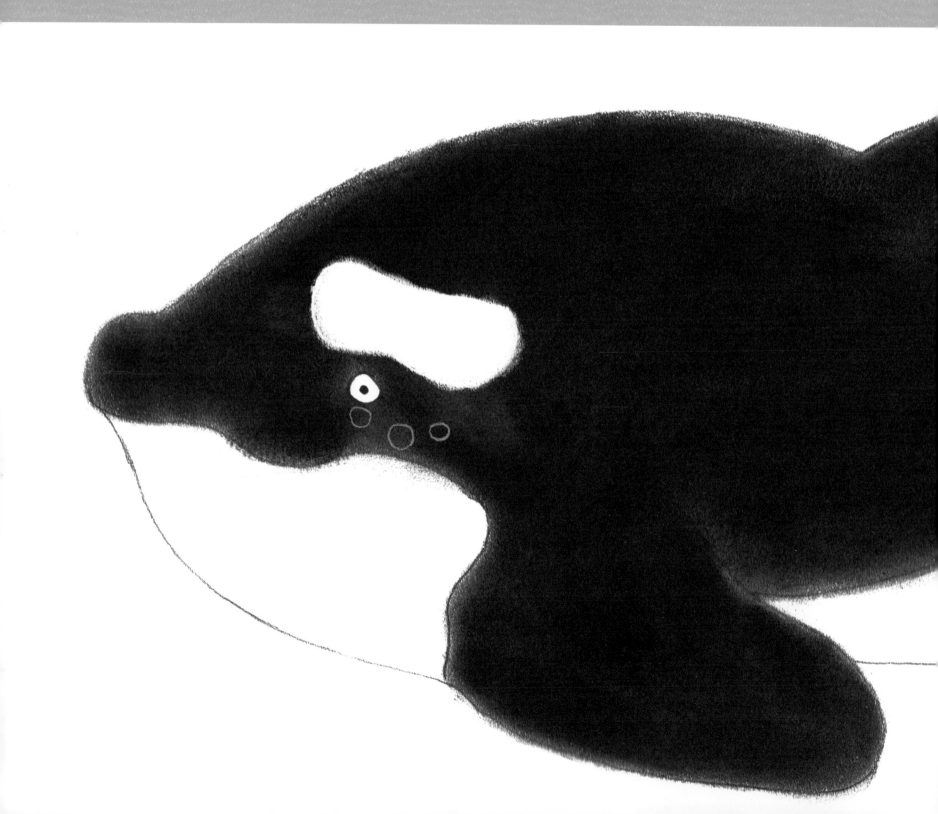

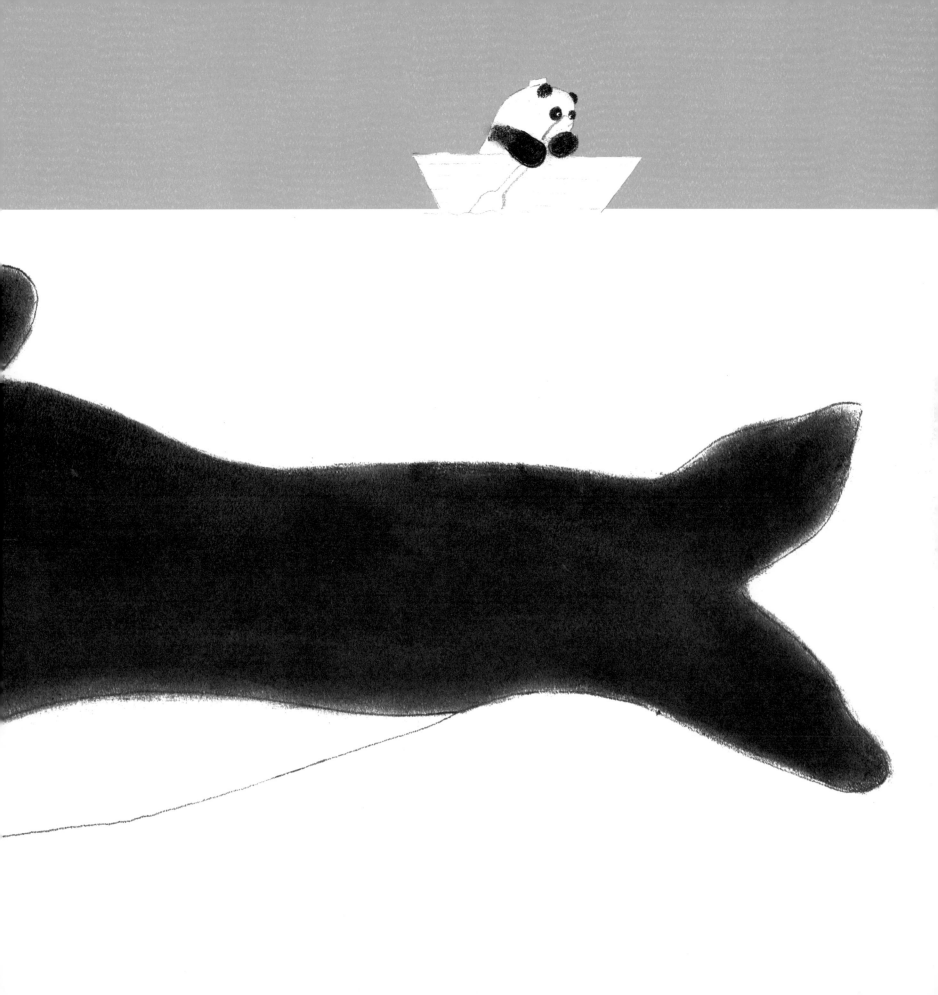

Would anyone else like a doughnut?

Hello!
May I have a doughnut...

PLEASE, Mr. Panda?

You can have them all.

Thank you
very much!

I love doughnuts.

You're welcome.
I do not like doughnuts.